What's the Time, Little Wolf?

Another Little Wolf and Smellybreff Adventure

How to play What's the Time, Mr. Wolf?

One player is Mr. Wolf. This player stands far from the others, facing away from them.
The other players call out, "What's the time, Mr. Wolf?"

If Mr. Wolf answers, "Five o' clock!" the players take five steps toward Mr. Wolf.
If the answer is "Twelve o'clock!" they take twelve steps, and so on.

When everyone is very close, Mr. Wolf answers, "Dinnertime!" The other players run
back to the start while Mr. Wolf chases them. Whoever is caught first is the next Mr. Wolf!
But if everyone makes it back to the start, the same player must be Mr. Wolf again.

E
WHY

For Ella Rose K and Teddy T
—I.W.

First American edition published in 2006 by Carolrhoda Books, Inc.

Text copyright © 2006 by Ian Whybrow
Illustrations copyright © 2006 by Tony Ross

Published by arrangement with HarperCollins Publishers Ltd., London, England. Originally published in English by
HarperCollins Publishers Ltd. under the title Little Wolf and Smellybreff: What's the Time, Little Wolf?

The author and artist assert the moral right to be identified as the author and artist of this work.

Carolrhoda Books, Inc.
A division of Lerner Publishing Group
241 First Avenue North
Minneapolis, MN 55401 U.S.A.

Website address: www.lernerbooks.com

Library of Congress Cataloging-in-Publication Data
Whybrow, Ian.
What's the time, Little Wolf? : another Little Wolf and Smellybreff adventure / by
Ian Whybrow ; illustrations by Tony Ross.— 1st American ed.
p.   cm.
Summary: Little Wolf and his brother Smellybreff play a naughty trick in their quest for dinner.
ISBN-13: 978–1–57505–939–6 (lib. bdg. : alk. paper)
ISBN-10: 1–57505–939–8 (lib. bdg. : alk. paper)
[1. Brothers—Fiction. 2. Wolves—Fiction.]
I. Ross, Tony, ill. II. Title. III. Title: What's the Time, Little Wolf?
PZ7.W6225Wgu 2006
[E]—dc22   2005031161

Printed and bound in Singapore
1 2 3 4 5 6 – OS – 11 10 09 08 07 06

What's the Time, Little Wolf?

Another Little Wolf and Smellybreff Adventure

Ian Whybrow + Tony Ross

Carolrhoda Books, Inc./Minneapolis

In a nice smelly lair, far away, lived the Wolf family.
They were all bad except for Little Wolf, and he
tried his hardest not to be good.
One day, not long before dinnertime, he was painting.
His baby brother was playing with his little drill and ax.

"Stop it, Smells!" said
Little Wolf. "Now you've made
me smudge my painting."

"Ow-wooooooo!"
howled Smellybreff.

"Gurr!" said Dad.
"Too noisy!
Go outside
and play!"

"Go on, Little," said Mom. "Take your baby brother and catch a nice, fat piggy for dinner."
"But Mom," said Little. "The piggies' house is miles away and you know Smells will keep moaning and asking what time it is."

"Out!" gurred Dad. "And don't come back with an empty sack!"

Little was right.
As soon as they were
out of the gate,
Smellybreff started.

"I'm hungry!" he moaned.
"When will we catch a piggy?"

"In a
MINUTE!"
said Little.

And when they reached
the lake, Smells was
still being a pain.

"I'm hungry!" he whined. "What's the time, Little Wolf?"

Just at that moment, Little spied a nest full of chicks.
"It's chicks o'clock!" he smiled.
"Time to catch some chicks for dinner!

We'll huff and we'll puff and we'll BLOW their nest down!"

But Smells didn't want to huff and puff. He wanted to chop with his little ax.

"Look out, chicks!" he shouted. "I will hop, I will plop, I will CHOP your house down!"

SPLASH!

went the chicks' nest,
into the lake.

"Ow-woooooo!" howled
Little Wolf and Smells.
"Now we're all wet and no
dinner in the sack!"

So on they went until Little spied some bees.
"I'm **HUNGRY!**" whined Smells. "What's the time, Little Wolf?"
Little Wolf said, "Don't worry, it's bee o'clock.
Time to collect some honey for dinner!

We'll huff and
we'll puff and
we'll BLOW their
hive down!"

But Smellybreff didn't
want to huff and puff.
He wanted to drill with
his little drill.

"Look out, bees!"
he shouted. "I will hill,
I will pill, I will DRILL
your house down!"

"Ow—woooooo!" howled Little Wolf and Smells.
"Now we're all wet and stung and STILL
no dinner in the sack!"

ZZZZZZZZZZZ

On they went,
tired and hungry. . .

until **AT LAST**. . .

. . .they reached
the piggies' house.

How the piggies laughed!
They sang:

"You two weaklings can't get in,
Not by the hair on your chinny-chin-chin!"

Poor Little Wolf! He did his best by huffing and puffing.
And Smellybreff did his best by drilling and chopping.
But they COULD NOT get in—not by the hair on their
chinny-chin-chin!

That did it.
Smells had a tantrum.

He howled,
"What's the time,
Little Wolf?

What's the time,
Little Wolf?

What's
the time,
Little Wolf?"

Just then, up popped lots of
nosy mice and rabbits.
"We like this game!" they
squeaked. "Can we play?"

"What a good idea!" said Little. "We'll stand here and cover our eyes. You have to wiggle up behind us VERY QUIETLY."

So the nosy mice and rabbits
wiggled up behind Little and Smells.

"What's the time,
Little Wolf?"
they wiggled.

"Fun o'clock!"
whispered Little
to Smells.

"What's the time,
Little Wolf?"

they jiggled.

"Chew o'clock,"
whispered Little.

"What's the time,
Little Wolf?"

they giggled.

"Dinnertime!"

shouted Little Wolf and Smells together.

And quick as a chick, their empty sack was FULL.

Dad was in a very good mood that evening.

"Lovely mice pies, Little!" he said.

"And fine rabbit rolls!" cooed Mom.

"Now tell me, was Smells a VERY bad cub today?"

. . . yum, yum!"